*Dedicated to my beloved family and to
Susan Tharpe's 1998-99 fourth grade class at
North Augusta Elementary School*

Christine Hurley Deriso

*To my wonderful wife Melissa,
thank you for all of your love, encouragement, and inspiration.
And to all of those who dare to follow their dreams*

Matthew Archambault

Dreams To Grow On

Written by Christine Hurley Deriso ✦ Illustrated by Matthew Archambault

ILLUMINATION
Arts

PUBLISHING COMPANY, INC.
BELLEVUE, WASHINGTON

The sun is up. The air is fresh. It's time to go and play.
Last night I dreamed of growing up and what I'll be someday.
A teacher? Or a doctor? Or a writer? Let me see…
Today I'll practice all the things I just might want to be.

I give a bottle to my doll and pat her when she's through,
then brush her silky hair and play a game of peek-a-boo.
She's learning how to walk—I hold her hand so she won't fall,
and dream that I'm a mother while I love my favorite doll.

Because my doll will need a house, I gather up my blocks
and build a cabin for her with a chimney made from rocks.
Though it's a little crooked, she is sure to understand,
'cause someday I might build the grandest house in all the land.

When snack time comes around, I mix some water with some dirt,
then top it off with clover for a wonderful dessert.
I dream about the day when I can bake real pies with cream.
I might become a baker, but today it's Mud Supreme.

My doll and I walk through the park to see what we can find.
I show her flowers, birds and insects, some of every kind.
I dream that I can study how the forest creatures grow.
Since I might be a scientist, there's lots for me to know.

And then I climb my monkey bars and wave from way up high.
I swing from bar to bar until my toes can touch the sky,
and dream about trapezes, soaring high up to the stars.
Yes, I might join the circus, so I'll start with monkey bars.

My father's in the garden, so I help him for a while.
I plant my seeds in little rows—that always makes him smile.
And if I tend my garden, I'll have lots of food to share.
I dream of growing vegetables for people everywhere.

And next I spread my arms like wings and make a humming sound,
then run around the yard and almost zoom up off the ground.
I dream that I can fly above the cities and the farms.
I might become a pilot, but today I'll use my arms.

I find my little brother and we climb our favorite tree.
Oh no, he fell! I'll save the day and bandage up his knee.
I dream about a time when I can save the lives of others.
I might become a doctor, so I'll start with little brothers.

I take him to a puddle where our boat can float around.
We might discover treasures there just waiting to be found.
I dream that I am sailing through a misty ocean breeze.
I might become a captain who explores the Seven Seas.

And now I try on dress-up clothes that Mommy used to wear,
with bracelets on my arms and frilly ribbons in my hair.
My friends are coming over, and we'll put on fancy shows.
Yes, I might be an actress, so I'll start with dress-up clothes.

For tea I go to Grandma's house and color while I'm there.
I draw a special picture, so she knows how much I care.
This drawing's just for Grandma, 'cause she really loves my style.
If I become an artist, I can make the whole world smile.

And then I visit friends of mine who've come from far off lands.
We may not look or talk alike, but we can all join hands.
We learn about each other as we find new games to play.
I might become a teacher, helping children every day.

The day is nearly over, so I snuggle in my chair,
imagining a girl who sprinkles stardust through the air.
She loves to have adventures—she is smart and brave and kind.
I might become a writer, so I'll start inside my mind.

A teacher? Or a doctor? Or a writer? Let me see…
I may just try them all. There are so many things to be.
My heart will lead the way, no matter what I choose to do.
Great things are sure to happen as I make my dreams come true.

ILLUMINATION

Arts

PUBLISHING COMPANY, INC.
P.O. Box 1865, Bellevue, WA 98009
Tel: 425-644-7185 ★ 888-210-8216 (orders only) ★ Fax: 425-644-9274
liteinfo@illumin.com ★ www.illumin.com

Library of Congress Cataloging-in-Publication Data

Deriso, Christine Hurley, 1961-
 Dreams to grow on / written by Christine Hurley Deriso ; illustrated by Matthew Archambault.
  p. cm.
 Summary: While playing, a little girl imagines a number of different things she might
grow up to be.
 ISBN 0-9701907-2-7 (hc)
 [1. Occupations—Fiction. 2. Play—Fiction. 3. Growth—Fiction. 4. Stories in rhyme.] I.
Archambault, Matthew, ill. II. Title.

PZ8.3.D4435 Dr 2002
[E]— dc21

                 2002024511

Published in the United States of America
Printed in Singapore by Star Standard Industries
Book Designer: Molly Murrah, Murrah & Company, Kirkland, WA

ILLUMINATION ARTS PUBLISHING COMPANY, INC.
is a member of Publishers in Partnership – replanting our nation's forests.

The Illumination Arts Collection Of Inspiring Children's Books

ALL I SEE IS PART OF ME by Chara M. Curtis, illustrated by Cynthia Aldrich
In this international bestseller, a child finds the light within his heart and his common link with all of life.

THE BONSAI BEAR by Bernard Libster, illustrated by Aries Cheung
Issa uses bonsai methods to keep his pet bear small, but the playful cub dreams of following its true nature.

CASSANDRA'S ANGEL by Gina Otto, illustrated by Trudy Joost
Cassandra feels lonely and misunderstood until a special angel guides her to the truth within.

CORNELIUS AND THE DOG STAR by Diana Spyropulos, illustrated by Ray Williams
Grouchy old Cornelius Basset-Hound can't enter Dog Heaven until he learns about love, fun and kindness.

THE DOLL LADY by H. Elizabeth Collins-Varni, illustrated by Judy Kuusisto
The doll lady teaches children to treat dolls kindly and with great love, for they are just like people.

DRAGON written and illustrated by Jody Bergsma
Born on the same day, a gentle prince and a ferocious, fire-breathing dragon share a prophetic destiny.

DREAMBIRDS by David Ogden, illustrated by Jody Bergsma
A Native American boy battles his own ego as he searches for the elusive dreambird and its powerful gift.

FUN IS A FEELING by Chara M. Curtis, illustrated by Cynthia Aldrich
Find your fun! "Fun isn't something or somewhere or who. It's a feeling of joy that lives inside of you."

HOW FAR TO HEAVEN? by Chara M. Curtis, illustrated by Alfred Currier
Exploring the wonders of nature, Nanna and her granddaughter discover that heaven is all around them.

LITTLE SQUAREHEAD by Peggy O'Neill, illustrated by Denise Freeman
Rosa overcomes the stigma of her unusual appearance after finding the glowing diamond within her heart.

THE LITTLE WIZARD written and illustrated by Jody Bergsma
Young Kevin discovers a wizard's cloak while on a perilous mission to save his mother's life.

ONE SMILE by Cindy McKinley, illustrated by Mary Gregg Byrne
Little Katie's innocent smile ignites a far-reaching circle of warmth and selfless giving.

THE RIGHT TOUCH by Sandy Kleven, LCSW, illustrated by Jody Bergsma
This award-winning, read-aloud story teaches children how to prevent sexual abuse.

SKY CASTLE by Sandra Hanken, illustrated by Jody Bergsma
Alive with dolphins, parrots and fairies, this magical tale inspires us to believe in the power of our dreams.

TO SLEEP WITH THE ANGELS by H. Elizabeth Collins, illustrated by Judy Kuusisto
Comforting her to sleep each night, a young girl's guardian angel fills her dreams with magical adventures.

THE TREE by Dana Lyons, illustrated by David Danioth
This powerful song of an ancient Douglas fir celebrates the age-old cycle of life in the Pacific Rain Forest.

WHAT IF... by Regina J. Williams, illustrated by Doug Keith
Using his fantastic imagination, a little boy delays bedtime for as long as possible. Glow-in-the-dark page included.

THE WHOOSH OF GADOOSH by Pat Skene, illustrated by Doug Keith
Gadoosh, a whimsical character without a home, inspires children to find the magic within their hearts.

WINGS OF CHANGE by Franklin Hill, Ph.D., illustrated by Aries Cheung
A contented little caterpillar resists his approaching transformation into a butterfly.

www.illumin.com